Apartment for rent

3

Orchard Books, A Grolier Company, 95 Madison Avenue, New York, NY 10016

Printed and bound by Phoenix Color Corp. Book design by Mina Greenstein
The text of this book is set in 16 point Caslon 224 Book. The illustrations are watercolor.

10 9 8 7 6 5 4 3 2 1

Library of Congress cataloging-in-publication data is available upon request.

ISBN 0-531-30307-1 (trade)   LC 00-25049
ISBN 0-531-33307-8 (library)

A Pig Is Moving In!

Claudia Fries

Orchard Books • New York

One morning, as Henrietta Hen was hanging out her wash, Doctor Fox greeted her with exciting news.

"A new neighbor is moving into our building today!"

"Oh, dear," said Henrietta. "I hope it is someone quiet and tidy."

Nick Hare popped his head out of the window. "A clean cat or an orderly mole would be nice. . . ."

Soon they heard the new tenant arriving.

Nick Hare, Doctor Fox, and Henrietta Hen all hid at the top of the stairs to get a glimpse of their new neighbor. When they saw him, they couldn't believe their eyes! He was not a clean cat; he was not an orderly mole; nor was he a fox, a hen, or a hare.

"Oh, my!" gasped Henrietta. "It's . . . a pig! A pig is moving in! That won't do at all. Everyone knows that pigs are messy and dirty and sloppy."

Doctor Fox and Nick Hare nodded in agreement.

Later that day, Doctor Fox met the pig carrying firewood. Doctor Fox walked by fast and didn't say hello, but he *did* slow down enough to see what the pig was up to. And he wasn't a bit surprised when the pig dropped some pieces of wood on the sidewalk.

Doctor Fox went to complain to Henrietta Hen.

"What a mess!" he said. "That pig has left wood all over our sidewalk."

"Oh, dear," said Henrietta.

She went out and looked, but she couldn't see any wood.

Doctor Fox must have swept it up, she thought.

But it was the pig who had swept up the mess. Then he went up to his apartment to build a nice warm fire.

Next it was Henrietta Hen's turn to meet the pig. He was carrying two heavy bags of groceries. She didn't say hello to him either, but she *did* sneak under the stairs to see what the pig would do this time. And she wasn't a bit surprised when he dropped a bag of flour at the bottom of the stairs. It burst open with a *puff* and a *splat*!

Henrietta Hen went to complain to Nick Hare.

"What a mess!" she said. "That pig has left our front hall covered in flour."

"How dreadful!" exclaimed Nick. He went out and looked, but he couldn't see any flour.

Henrietta must have cleaned it up, he thought.

But it was the pig who had swept and mopped the floor. Then he went into his kitchen to bake cinnamon cookies.

Not long after, Nick Hare met the pig. He walked slowly behind the pig so that he wouldn't have to say hello, but he *did* wait to see what would happen. He couldn't believe his eyes: the pig was carrying mud into his apartment! The mud was dripping all over the floor, and the pig walked right through it, leaving a trail of hoofprints behind him.

Nick Hare went to complain to Doctor Fox and Henrietta Hen. "What a mess!" he said. "That pig has left mud all over our stairs!"

"Disgusting!" agreed Doctor Fox and Henrietta Hen, shaking their heads. But when they went out and looked, they couldn't see any mud.

"Nick must have cleaned it up," they said.

But it was the pig who had scrubbed the stairs three times over. And it wasn't mud—it was clay. The pig was taking it up to his workshop to make pottery.

"That does it," declared Henrietta, Nick, and Doctor Fox. "If a pig wants to live in our building, he must behave properly. Otherwise, he will have to go!"

And they marched upstairs to tell him.

They rang the doorbell.
Dingdong! Dingdong! Dingdong!

"Oh . . . hello!" said the pig.
He was surprised to have visitors
so soon.

Doctor Fox, Henrietta Hen, and Nick Hare were about
to complain when the door opened wider. A sweet smell of
cinnamon floated out, and they heard a fire crackling in the
pig's living room.

"We noticed a mess in the hallway—" began Doctor Fox.

"Oh, I *do* apologize," said the pig, "and I hope I've cleaned
everything up thoroughly."

Doctor Fox, Henrietta Hen, and Nick Hare looked at one
another in surprise.

"So it wasn't you who swept
up the wood!" said Henrietta to
Doctor Fox.

"And it wasn't you who
cleaned up the flour!" said
Nick to Henrietta.

"And it wasn't you who
washed away the muddy
hoofprints!" said Doctor Fox
and Henrietta to Nick.

Very embarrassed, they realized that the pig had cleaned everything up himself.

"My name is Theodore," said the pig. "Will you join me for tea?"

So they did. Doctor Fox, Henrietta Hen, and Nick Hare went into Theodore's bright, clean kitchen and helped him set out tea and cookies. They admired all the cups and pots he had made in his workshop.

"I have a new game we could play," said Theodore. When he got it out, Henrietta was flattered to see that he had made a special playing piece for each of his new neighbors.

"You have a lovely apartment, Theodore," said Nick Hare, biting into another cookie.

"It's a beautiful place," echoed Doctor Fox and Henrietta Hen. They were happily imagining all the cozy afternoons they were going to spend together.

What a wonderful new neighbor they had!